THIS BOOK Belongs to ....

Frontispiece

The Night Before Christmas

BY
CLEMENT C. MOORE

With Twenty-eight Illustrations

APPLEWOOD BOOKS
BEDFORD, MASSACHUSETTS

This edition of *The Night Before Christmas* was originally published in 1918.
This book has been reproduced from a copy at the Brown University Library. Applewood Books would like to thank the Brown University Library for their permission to reprint this book.

ISBN 1-55709-410-1

Thank you for purchasing an Applewood Book. Applewood reprints America's lively classics—books from the past that are of interest to modern readers. For a free copy of our current catalog, write to: Applewood Books, 18 North Road, Bedford, MA 01730.

Printed and bound in Singapore

Library of Congress Cataloging-in-Publication Data:
Moore, Clement Clarke, 1779-1863.
    The night before Christmas / by Clement C. Moore.
        p.   cm.
    This edition was originally published in 1918.
    ISBN 1-55709-410-1
    1. Santa Claus—juvenile poetry.   2. Christmas—juvenile
poetry.   3. Children's poetry, American.   I. Title.
PS2429.M5N5   1995b
811'.2 – dc20   95-20326
                                                        CIP

THE NIGHT BEFORE CHRISTMAS

'TWAS the night before
  Christmas,
When all through the
  house,
Not a creature was stirring,
  Not even a mouse;

THE stockings were hung
By the chimney with
care,
In hopes that St. Nicholas
Soon would be there;

THE children were nestled
    All snug in their beds,
While visions of sugar-plums
Danced in their heads;

A<small>ND</small> Mamma in her
kerchief
And I in my cap,
Had just settled our heads
For a long winter's nap—

WHEN out on the lawn
There rose such a
clatter,
I sprang from my bed
To see what was the matter;

AWAY to the window
   I flew like a flash,
   Tore open the shutters
And threw up the sash.

THE moon, on the breast
Of the new-fallen snow,
Gave a lustre of mid-day
To objects below;

WHEN what to my won-
dering eyes should
appear,
But a miniature sleigh,
And eight tiny Reindeer;

WITH a little old driver,
  So lively and quick,
I knew in a moment
  It must be St. Nick;

MORE rapid than eagles
His coursers they
came,
And he whistled, and
shouted,
And called them by name—

"NOW Dasher! now
Dancer!
Now Prancer! and Vixen!
On Comet! on Cupid!
On Dunder! and Blitzen!

TO the top of the porch!
    To the top of the wall!
Now, dash away, dash away,
    Dash away, all!"

AS dry leaves that before
The wild hurricane
fly,
When they meet with an
obstacle,
Mount to the sky;

SO, up to the house-top
    The coursers they flew,
With sleigh full of toys—
    And St. Nicholas too.

AND then in a twinkling
I heard on the roof
The prancing and pawing
Of each little hoof;

AS I drew in my head,
   And was turning
      around,
Down the chimney St.
   Nicholas
   Came with a bound

HE was dressed all in fur
   From his head to his
      foot;
And his clothes were all
      tarnished
   With ashes and soot;

ABUNDLE of toys
    He had flung on his
        back,
And he looked like a
        peddler
Just opening his pack;

HIS eyes how they
twinkled!
His dimples how merry,
His cheeks were like roses,
His nose like a cherry;

41

HIS droll little mouth
    Was drawn up like a
        bow,
And the beard on his chin
    Was as white as the snow!

THE stump of a pipe
He held tight in his
teeth,
And the smoke, it encircled
His head like a wreath.

45

HE had a broad face,
   And a little round
      belly,
That shook when he
      laughed,
Like a bowl-full of jelly.

HE was chubby and
        plump,
A right jolly old elf,
And I laughed when I saw
        him,
In spite of myself.

A WINK of his eye,
　　And a twist of his
　　　　head,
Soon gave me to know
　　I had nothing to dread.

H E spoke not a word,
   But went straight to
   his work,
And filled all the stock-
   ings,
   Then turned with a jerk,

AND laying his finger
Aside of his nose,
And giving a nod,
Up the chimney he rose.

HE sprang to his sleigh,
  To his team gave a
    whistle,
And away they all flew,
Like the down of a thistle;

BUT I heard him exclaim
    Ere he drove out of
        sight,
  "Merry Christmas to all,
And to all a Good Night!"

THE
END

WEE BOOKS FOR WEE FOLK
- *The Night Before Christmas* •
- *A Child's Garden of Verses* •
- *Slovenly Betsy* •